STUART LITTLE™

A Columbia Pictures Presentation

Stuart's New Brother

Based on the screenplay
by M. Night Shyamalan and Greg Brooker

AVON BOOKS
An Imprint of HarperCollins*Publishers*

COLUMBIA PICTURES PRESENTS
A DOUGLAS WICK AND FRANKLIN/WATERMAN PRODUCTION A FILM BY ROB MINKOFF GEENA DAVIS "STUART LITTLE" HUGH LAURIE AND JONATHAN LIPNICKI
MUSIC BY ALAN SILVESTRI EXECUTIVE PRODUCERS JEFF FRANKLIN AND STEVE WATERMAN AND JASON CLARK BASED ON THE BOOK BY E.B. WHITE SCREENPLAY BY M. NIGHT SHYAMALAN AND GREG BROOKER
PRODUCED BY DOUGLAS WICK DIRECTED BY ROB MINKOFF

www.stuartlittle.com

COLUMBIA PICTURES

Stuart's New Brother

Adaptation by Leslie Goldman

Printed in the United States of America.
For information address HarperCollins Children's Books, a division of HarperCollins Publishers, 1350 Avenue of the Americas, New York, NY 10019.

Library of Congress Catalog Card Number: 00-104181
ISBN 0-06-444290-X

First Avon edition, 2000

AVON TRADEMARK REG. U.S. PAT. OFF. AND IN OTHER COUNTRIES,
MARCA REGISTRADA, HECHO EN U.S.A.

❖

www.stuartlittle.com
www.harperchildrens.com

Stuart wanted to play.
So he went to find
his new brother, George.

He found George
in the basement,
playing with his toys.
"Wow," said Stuart.
"It's the Wild West."

"Did you build all these?"
Stuart asked George.
"My dad and I did,"
said George.

SHERIFF
BANK

Stuart strutted
around the town.
"It's like living
in a real live Western.
Howdy, partner,"
said Stuart.

"I'm trying to concentrate!"
said George.
"Oh, sorry," said Stuart.
"Is that a train?"

"What does it look like,
Picklehead?"
asked George.
"Can we play with it?
Please?"
begged Stuart.

Minutes later,
Stuart was on the tracks.
The train was speeding
toward him.
"Help me!"
he yelled.

The train got closer and closer.
Stuart unraveled his tail

from around his body.
He jumped off the tracks.

George and
Stuart laughed.
"You're crazy!"
said George.

Stuart noticed a giant model boat.
"What's that?" he asked.
"That's the *Wasp*,"
said George.

"She's beautiful,"
said Stuart.
"Yeah, but she's not finished,"
said George.

“When are you
going to finish it?”
asked Stuart.
“Well, my dad and I
were building her, but…
I decided to stop,”
said George.

"How come?" asked Stuart.
"I'm too little
for a race like that,"
said George.
"You're not too little,"
said Stuart.

George shook his head.
"You've never seen
one of these races.
Everyone from school is there.
What if I lost?"

“At least you will have tried.
Come on, George.
Let’s get started,” said Stuart.
“You know, I always wanted
a brother,” said George.

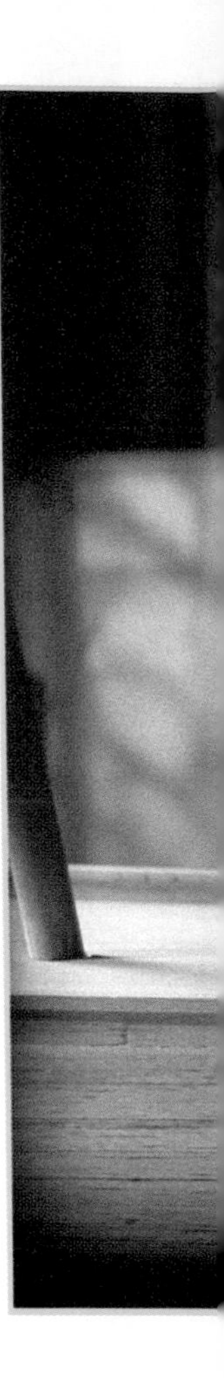

"Can a brother be a friend, too?"
asked Stuart.
"That's the best kind,"
said George.